SUPER FLY

FLY

Rise of the
Evil Army!

The Super Fly series

SUPER FLY

Rise of the Evil Army!

Todd H. Doodler

BLOOMSBURY

NEW YORK LONDON OXFORD NEW DELHI SYDNEY

First published in the United States of America in February 2017
by Bloomsbury Children's Books
www.bloomsbury.com

Bloomsbury is a registered trademark of Bloomsbury Publishing Plc

For information about permission to reproduce selections from this book, write to
Permissions, Bloomsbury Children's Books, 1385 Broadway, New York, New York 10018
Bloomsbury books may be purchased for business or promotional use. For information
on bulk purchases please contact Macmillan Corporate and Premium Sales Department at
specialmarkets@macmillan.com

Library of Congress Cataloging-in-Publication Data
Names: Doodler, Todd H., author, illustrator.
Title: Rise of the evil army / by Todd H. Doodler.
Description: New York : Bloomsbury, 2017. | Series: Super Fly ; 4
Summary: Super Fly has stopped Crazy Cockroach from taking over the world. He's
conquered an entire hypnotized city of bugs. He's even battled his own sidekick!
But now Super Fly is facing the most dangerous threat of all:
an evil army of insects organized by Crazy Cockroach himself.
Identifiers: LCCN 2016013307 (print) | LCCN 2016036823 (e-book)
ISBN 978-1-61963-387-2 (paperback) • ISBN 978-1-61963-388-9 (hardcover)
ISBN 978-1-61963-389-6 (e-book)
Subjects: | CYAC: Superheroes—Fiction. | Flies—Fiction. | Insects—Fiction.
Humorous stories. | BISAC: JUVENILE FICTION/Humorous Stories. |
JUVENILE FICTION/Action & Adventure/General. |
JUVENILE FICTION/Comics & Graphic Novels/Superheroes.
Classification: LCC PZ7.D7247 Ri 2017 (print) | LCC PZ7.D7247 (e-book) |
DDC [Fic]—dc23
LC record available at https://lccn.loc.gov/2016013307

Book design by Nicole Gastonguay and Yelena Safronova
Printed and bound in the U.S.A. by Berryville Graphics Inc., Berryville, Virginia
2 4 6 8 10 9 7 5 3 1 (paperback)
2 4 6 8 10 9 7 5 3 1 (hardcover)

All papers used by Bloomsbury Publishing, Inc., are natural, recyclable products
made from wood grown in well-managed forests. The manufacturing processes
conform to the environmental regulations of the country of origin.

To my favorite superhero of them all, my daughter, Electrifying Elle!

CONTENTS

A Very Super Fly

Eugene Flystein had never been an ordinary fly. Sure, he liked buzzing around and eating poop and smelly garbage. But Eugene also loved inventing things.

So far, his most successful invention was the Ultimo 6-9000. The Ultimo looked and tasted like key lime pie. Its name came from the fact that in a mere six seconds the pseudo-pie made whoever ate it 9,000 times smarter, faster, and more powerful.

After just one bite, Eugene was

transformed from a clumsy, slow-flying fourth grader into . . . **SUPER FLY**!

At first, Eugene's best friend, Fred Flea, chose not to consume the dessert of destiny. But he did agree to help Eugene as his non-super sidekick, **FANTASTIC FLEA**.

When Eugene's younger sister, Elle, tasted the Ultimo 6-9000, she became **FLY GIRL**. And it's a good thing, too, because without Fly Girl's help Eugene and Fred might never have defeated Cornelius C. Roach, the bully who bit the pie to become the super villain, Crazy Cockroach. Yes, that's a lot of superpower pie eating, I know.

Later, Fred ate the Ultimo 6-9000 and even shared some with a feisty flea named Fiona. Thanks to some tricky pranks arranged by Crazy Cockroach, Fred briefly became the villain Furious Flea before returning to the good side. He resumed his friendship with the Flysteins and was once again known as **FANTASTIC FLEA**.

Eugene and Elle were glad to have the now-super Fred back in the good leg of their dirty-diaper headquarters. Crazy Cockroach and his henchbugs, Dee and Doo Dung, had headquarters (complete with refrigerator and Ping-Pong table) in the other leg.

If you're wondering why you haven't seen any of this craziness on the news, it's because all of this took place in the bug-centric town of Stinkopolis. And frankly, we don't get that news channel. In that dump swarming with insects was an old toilet bowl in which floated Brown Barge Elementary School. This is where all these insect kids go to school—students by day and superheroes/villains after school.

If you want the details, please read

the first three books, which describe Eugene's amazing adventures. Otherwise, let's join our heroes—and villains—in progress!

1

Danger in the Forecast

One fine fall afternoon, Elle Flystein felt an extra chill in the air, the chill of trouble. Fall leaves crashed on the junk cluttering the stinking streets of Stinkopolis.

As they walked home from the bus stop, Elle; her brother, Eugene; and his best friend, Fred, deftly dodged the brightly colored hazards easily a hundred times their size.

Eugene and Fred laughed and laughed so hard that Elle had to ask, "What're you laughing at?"

Eugene looked at Fred. The athletic flea shrugged.

Eugene pushed up his eyeglasses and then . . . burst out laughing.

Fred laughed too. "We don't remember."

Elle shook her head, but she couldn't help smiling at seeing her brother and Fred acting like pest friends again. For a while, Fred had been seduced by the Dark Side of the Diaper.

To be fair, the trouble started with Eugene. After being named Brown Barge's Student of the Season, Eugene started acting too cool for school, and he was too busy for his best pal.

So Fred fell for a pretty flea named

Fiona, and worse, he started hanging out with Cornelius C. Roach and those dumb beetles, Dee and Doo Dung. Lots of good bugs do bad things under the influence of bad friends.

Fred became a super villain! Now the boys acted like the whole crazy thing had never happened.

At least Eugene wasn't acting like Mr. Big Bug on Campus anymore. That was more annoying than an ant with ants in his pants. And

 after school at the Flysteins' home or in the good leg of the diaper, the boys were back

 on Wi-Fly playing *Sewer Invaders*, practicing their

 superhero moves, or working on Eugene's latest invention.

A cool breeze made Elle's wings flutter and her spine shudder. The 9,000-times-more-intelligent second grader wasn't just cold. Her super brain kept calculating the likelihood of Crazy Cockroach making another outlandish attempt to defeat Super Fly and take over the world. And the answer was always the same—a hundred percent likely.

Super villains live for revenge and world domination. Crazy Cockroach was a super villain. Therefore . . . it only became a question of when and how.

By the time Elle arrived at that thought, the friends had reached the Flystein home. Eugene told Elle, "We finally remembered what we were laughing about."

Fred nodded but didn't speak for fear of cracking up.

Elle tapped one foot on the ground. "Well?"

Eugene sputtered through helpless giggles. "We were laughing about how we can't stop laughing."

Elle wanted to tell them, "Hey! Remember, we're superheroes. Any second now we might need to save the world again." But she was laughing too hard.

2

The Con Is Coming!

The phone rang before Eugene had a chance
to open the refrigerator and look for something disgusting to eat.

Adam Aphid chattered breathlessly on
the other end. "Did you see the notice?"

Eugene felt clueless.
"What notice?"

Adam's squeal nearly
shattered Eugene's
eyeglasses. "Comic Con's
coming to Stinkopolis!"

Eager to hear every exciting word, Fred hopped around Eugene.

Elle ran to pick up the extension in their parents' bedroom. She squealed, "*The* Comic Con?"

Adam sighed. "Well, no, but *a* Comic Con. Isn't that thrilling enough?"

Elle squealed. "You bet it is!"

Eugene said, "Send me the link, and we'll talk later!"

Adam chuckled. "Okay, over and out, or whatever, dude!"

Now, every bug knew Bug Con is the biggest comic book and superhero convention around. Unless they've been living under a rock or sleeping in a cocoon, that is.

The phone rang again, even before Eugene could power up his computer. Carlos Caterpillar also

11

wanted to know if the friends knew about the Con.

Eugene snapped, "I'd know more if I could visit this link and . . ."

The link from Adam filled in with a flashing banner proclaiming, "Stinkopolis's first and best Bug-Con!"

Fred and Elle crushed Eugene from either side as his 9,000-times-enhanced eyes and brain took in the announcement.

"A real con!" Eugene exclaimed.

"Free admission!" Fred added.

Elle squealed. "Ooh! There's a super-hero/villain costume contest!"

Eugene and Fred loved costumes. They were always coming up with funny duo-bug costumes, like "spider and web" or "dog poop and fly" (which was especially funny because Fred dressed as the fly and Eugene, the poop). Of course, their favorite costumes were Super Fly and Fantastic  Flea. But those really weren't costumes, those were work uniforms.

Elle's super brain reached the same thought at the same time. So all three super-bugs exclaimed, "We can dress as ourselves!"

Elle giggled. "We'll be the only ones who get the joke."

3

Comic Con—
Stinkopolis Style

Word of the upcoming Comic Con spread through Brown Barge Elementary School faster than bug flu in February. Everybug wanted a chance to shop for comics, attend panels to discuss serious issues (like whether MegaMoth could beat SuperSlug in a one-on-one fight) and browse tables full of cool T-shirts and promotional

freebies. All of that—along with meeting their real-life superheroes hoping to score an autograph or selfie with them—was enough to set the halls abuzz.

Many bugs debated the merits of various costumes and whether to enter the contest or just vote for the best.

Lucy Kaboosie fretted, "I can't believe we only have three days to get ready." The lovely ladybug enjoyed costume contests but worried that she wouldn't have enough time to prep a winning entry.

Ted Tarantula agreed. "It's not like you can go to BugMart and buy a Super Fly costume."

His friend Sid Spider said, "I'd rather dress as Fantastic Flea." Then he shrugged. "Either way we'll have to hide two of our legs."

Eugene nudged Fred. As usual, Fred knew what his friend was thinking: How cool is it to be the subject for a costume?

Cornelius C. Roach also found the discussion amusing. After all, the secret super villain was behind the Con!

As he'd told Dee and Doo on the evil side of the diaper the other day, "Super Fly and Fantastic Flea both love comic books, making a Con the perfect trap!"

"A con Con!" Crazy Cockroach giggled.

The Dungs didn't get it, but laughed along anyway. They were far from the brightest bugs at Brown Barge, so Cornelius had to explain. "It's just the place to stage a fight between heroes."

Dee still didn't understand.

Cornelius went on, "Eugene and Fred both want the rare *Poo Poo* #2 issue. I'll arrange to have one copy at the Con and . . ."

Doo's lonely, lazy brain cells struggled to spark. "Uh, so Super Fly and Fantastic Flea will fight over the comic book?"

Cornelius sighed. "Yes!"

Dee scratched his head. "But I heard Fred and Eugene vowed never to let any-thing come between them again."

Cornelius cackled. "That was before they saw a copy of *Poo Poo* #2." His eyes lit with evil glee. "And while those 'pest friends' fight, we'll flatter Elle into thinking that she's the greatest hero since Hercules. And why does she need to play second fly to Super Fly? Then, before you can say 'sucker!', she'll be our friend, just like Fred was . . ."

"Until he turned good again," Dee pointed out.

Cornelius glared.

Doo clamped a hand over his brother's mouth.

Dee mumbled, "Just sayin'."

Then the villain and his dimwitted sidekicks got busy ordering tables, posting a website, and otherwise making Stinkopolis's first and best Con a reality.

Under the Big Tent

On the big day, on the good side of the diaper, Eugene, Fred, and Elle quivered with excitement.

Elle giggled. "This is so much fun! I thought I'd have to wait till I was old enough to go to Bug Diego for the big convention, or at least Swamp City. It's so great to have a Con right here in Stinkopolis!"

Eugene admired himself in the mirror. "I usually worry about someone recognizing that Super Fly is Eugene Flystein.

Today I just have to look awesome."

Fred shook his head. "Uh-oh. Sounds like the Big Bug on Campus might be coming back."

Eugene quickly assured him. "No way, best buddy. I'm only as big as my friendship with you."

Elle glanced at her watch. "The doors open in ten minutes. Let's go!"

The three super friends could've flown to the convention location in less than three seconds. But they didn't want to blow their cover and let everyone know that they were the real Super Fly, Fly Girl, and Fantastic Flea. So they strolled to the site, along with a crowd that seemed to include every bug in Brown Barge. Even some of the adult bugs were in costume. Being a superhero fan isn't just for kids, ya know.

Eugene felt flattered to see lots of other bugs dressed as Super Fly. Big Butch Recluse looked pretty silly stuffed into the costume, especially with two of his legs tied behind his back. And it was especially cool to see the cute little larvae and baby bugs dressed as mini Super Flies.

Lucy Kaboosie's Fly Girl costume looked almost as good as Elle's!

Jeremy Cricket's Fantastic Flea outfit looked

like a toddler had drawn it on an old T-shirt. But the cricket could hop almost as high as the real hero.

The dressed-up superheroes came in all shapes and sizes, but as our real superheroes know, being a superhero is more than just a cool costume.

The convention was being held under

four human-sized comic books balanced on top of soda-bottle support poles.

Lucy shouted, "Eugene, is that really you?"

Eugene felt glad his mask hid his embarrassment, as he stammered, "No, it's Super Fly!"

Lucy laughed. "Right, and I'm Fly Girl!"

Elle laughed too. "No, I'm Fly Girl!"

Then the two girls danced around each other giggling with glee. "We're both Fly Girl!"

Lucy said, "I hope we both win the contest!"

"Impossible," a voice near them asserted.

The girls turned and saw . . . Crazy Cockroach!

"Great costume!" Lucy exclaimed.

Elle blinked. She knew that costume, and . . . it wasn't exactly a costume. Thanks to her 9,000-times-enhanced powers of observation, Elle knew that the roach dressed as Crazy Cockroach was indeed Cornelius C. Roach—the real Crazy Cockroach!

The villain bowed. "Thank you."

Elle's eyes narrowed, and her brain raced. Hearing Cornelius be  polite made her spine tingle. Surely the roach was up to something, but what?

Elle added up the facts. Cornelius was at the Con. Almost every young bug in Stinkopolis was there too. So he was dressed as his alter ego—well, so were she, Eugene, and Fred. What could it mean?

Crazy Cockroach smiled. Elle shuddered at the mirthless display of roach mouth parts. "Did you make that costume yourself?" he asked.

Elle nodded.

"You're amazing! I knew you were smart,

but I had no idea you were so talented too," the roach gushed.

Elle felt her breakfast rising. She liked compliments as much as the next bug, but when they came from a villain like Cornelius . . .

Just then, the Dungs rushed up with a plateful of fragrant snacks. "I love fried scabs!" Dee exclaimed.

"Want some?" Doo held out the plate to Elle.

The scabs did smell delicious, but Elle remained suspicious.

Dee ate one, and then Doo. They didn't die, or even gag.

Cornelius chuckled warmly. "See? Not poisoned, just fattening. But we understand if you want to keep your perfect physique."

Elle blushed. "Oh, I'm far from perfect."

"Really?" Cornelius asked. "Not from

here. It seems to me you're a strong young fly with everything going for her: great look, great powers, even great shoes."

Elle looked down at her shoes. They *were* great! But it still didn't feel great to have Cornelius say nice things to her.

Doo pushed the plate closer to Elle.

Dee took another scab and crunched it loudly. "Yum, yum."

Elle shook her head. "You're not fooling me. I know you're just acting friendly as part of some evil plot. You weren't my friends before, and you aren't going to suddenly become my friends now."

Pure fury flashed across the cockroach's face. He wanted to smash the clever young fly right then and there. But he had his secret identity to protect. Besides, he also had to check on his scheme against Elle's brother and Fred.

So Crazy Cockroach made his way to

the trading tables, specifically to the one in possession of the rare *Poo Poo* #2. As he approached the table, Cornelius felt pleased to see Eugene and Fred engaged in a serious conversation.

Eugene held the comic book carefully by the edge of the plastic bag protecting it. He said, "You saw it first."

Fred protested, "But you've always been more of a *Poo Poo* fan than me."

Cornelius blinked. Something wasn't right. The friends were arguing, but where were the punches, the insults, the karate kicks below the belt?

The two pest friends just disagreed

amicably. They were being polite and cordial. This made the roach sick to his stomach.

Eugene's voice rose. "Are you serious? You love *Poo Poo* too!"

"Okay, I'll buy it," Fred conceded. Then he muttered, "But you can't stop me from giving it to you for your birthday."

"I'll pay half," Eugene insisted. "Then we can share."

To Crazy Cockroach's complete disgust, the two heroes then shook hands and grinned.

"That's a deal," Eugene declared.

"You can read it first," Fred offered.

Eugene shook his head. "We'll read it out loud—together!"

Crazy Cockroach almost puked in his mouth. Instead, he took his anger out on his minions. "It's all your fault!" he told the Dungs.

"Really?" Doo wondered.

"How?" Dee asked.

Crazy Cockroach didn't bother to explain. He just kicked the soda-bottle supports until the comic books collapsed on the costumed bugs. As everyone scrambled out of the fallen tent, the roach cackled.

Then he commanded, "To the diaper!" And the Dungs rushed to keep up with their super-bossy boss.

Jeremy's Jitters

Back in the evil side of the diaper, Cornelius sulked. "So much for causing those disgusting 'pest buddies' to fight—or getting Elle to fall for false friendship."

Dee shrugged. "You did your best."

Doo added, "You almost crushed an ant with one of those soda bottles."

"Yeah," Dee hastily agreed. "And everybug was disappointed about the contest."

Doo sighed. "I was hoping we'd win!"

Cornelius punched the wall in frustration. But, of course, it was so cottony-soft his super fist tore through it with ease.

The Dungs cowered in the corner, afraid of becoming Crazy Cockroach's next target.

Instead, the villain bounced a Ping-Pong ball across the table, then raced to bounce it back to himself, and so on until both Dungs felt dizzy.

Finally, Cornelius fell back down onto the couch, exhausted. "Maybe we need to bully weaker bugs to work out some of the  kinks," he mused. "Then we'll come up with a better way to get Super Fly."

The Dungs quickly agreed. They liked any plan that didn't involve Crazy Cockroach punching them.

"Yeah, tomorrow's another day," Dee pointed out.

"And those three superbugs aren't the only victims at Brown Barge," Doo added.

Cornelius sighed. "You sound like the introduction to *Bullying for Dummies*."

Dee grinned. "Really?"

Doo smiled too. "No one ever said I sounded like a book before."

Cornelius turned away and wrote on his Top Secret To-Do List: *Find smarter henchbugs.*

The next morning, Eugene, Elle, and Fred saw a new bug on the bus. She was a tall, pretty wasp who stung six bugs before they even reached the next stop.

"Ow!"

"Ow!"

"Hey!"

"Ouch!"

"What the . . ."

"YIKES!"

"Who are you?" Adam Aphid asked.

"Hoops Hornet," she replied. "Probably the best bugsketball player you'll ever meet. Definitely the toughest."

Eugene nudged Fred and whispered, "Wow! She's even meaner than Cornelius!"

Adam said, "Hoops, huh. Is that because you love bugsketball, or is that your real name?"

The tall hornet laughed. "Well it's not because I like hula hoops." Then she sternly answered, "Both."

Then her eyes narrowed as she caught Fred staring at her. Hoops stared back and wouldn't stop. The stare turned into a glare that gave the poor flea goose bumps. Goose bumps on a flea are like mumps on a person. Fred felt bad!

Hoops went on to spread misery for the rest of the day. In science lab, the tough hornet seemed very smart, but also mean.  When Willie Weevil called her "Poops," Hoops stuck his head in a beaker and held it over a Bunsen burner until he cried uncle.

Eugene said, "Please excuse Willie. He thinks he's a witty weevil, and he's really just lame. Most Brown Barge students aren't so rude to new bugs."

Hoops shrugged. "Who cares? I can hold my own."

Eugene backed away, fearing that his ferocious new classmate might decide to put *his* head in a beaker and turn the burner up to high.

That should've been enough excitement for one day. Instead, right in the middle of the math lesson, the strangest thing happened: Jeremy Cricket snapped!

First he started mumbling to himself about hundreds too many larvae in the nest and not enough grass to go around.

Then the substitute teacher, Miss Spider, looked concerned. "Jeremy, please raise your . . ."

Jeremy didn't even notice her. His voice just grew louder and louder, and the sentences stopped making sense. Single words rose out of a sea of angry sounds: siblings, homework, bullies, bicycle, noise, pressure, math, and chores.

Miss Spider tried again. "Jeremy Cricket, you know better than to talk without raising your . . ."

Jeremy raised his arms, but not to ask

permission to speak. He used them to turn over his desk! **BANG!**

Then the furious cricket ate his pencil. He threw his glasses against the wall and emptied out his backpack on the floor.

And when Miss Spider tried to lead him toward the door, he started to arm wrestle with her! It's never a good idea to arm wrestle someone with eight arms.

Miss Spider soon had poor Jeremy wrapped up in a tidy silk package bound for Principal Praying Mantis's office. Then she quickly returned to Mrs. Tiger Moth's lesson plan.

But everyone in the class felt a bit freaked out, including Eugene and Fred. While they waited for the final bell to ring, the super-bugs mused upon the strange incident.

So did Cornelius C. Roach. The villain wondered what would make a decent bug like Jeremy go all buggy. He decided to find Jeremy and ask.

At first, Eugene suspected foul play, mostly because that would give Super Fly a chance to do some detective work. But after reviewing the events in his mind, Eugene concluded, "The poor cricket was probably exhausted, maybe stressed out from drama at home, or just picked on once too often."

Fred agreed.

So while Cornelius looked for Jeremy, the heroes simply boarded the bus for home.

The roach found the now-subdued cricket leaving the principal's office. The secretary, Mrs. Mosca, gave Jeremy a tissue to blow his nose. Chubby Mrs. Mosca patted his shoulder and reassured him, "Everything will be fine. You'll see. And if it isn't, you can always stop by and talk. Mr. Mantis's door is always open. I'm here too."

Mrs. Mosca buzzed with surprise as a smiling Cornelius approached Jeremy. She hoped the bully wouldn't tease the already stressed-out cricket.

She felt relieved when Cornelius asked, "Are you okay?"

Jeremy nodded. But he also felt confused by the cockroach's friendly manner.

"Are you sure?" Cornelius went on in a gentle tone. "I've never seen you act like that before."

Jeremy would've blushed if his ichor wasn't clear. As it was, the embarrassed cricket looked down at the floor. "Yeah,

well, there's a lot going on at home right now. Hundreds of new siblings just hatched. And last week my bicycle was stolen, so I haven't been able to go riding, which is my favorite way to just forget everything and relax."

Cornelius chuckled to himself. Dee and Doo had stolen that bike under his direction. Not that they needed it, but hey, you can't call yourself a super villain without doing mean things.

Jeremy's antennae drooped as he droned on, "The construction project near our house is so noisy I haven't been getting much sleep. So my nerves are totally frayed."

The cricket looked at the roach nervously. Why was Cornelius even talking to him? Usually the bully just started punching or giving him wedgies. Instead, he wore the mask of a caring friend.

"That's too bad," Cornelius said gently.

Jeremy sighed. "I guess I lost control for a minute there. I just wanted to tear the world apart! I'm really sorry. That's not like me at all."

Cornelius nodded. "Of course not." Then he muttered to himself, "Stress and pressure add up to . . . a good bug gone bad!"

Cornelius's 9,000-times-enhanced intellect raced with theories. If circumstance could create a crazed cricket, could Crazy Cockroach somehow simulate those same forces . . . ? Surely he could make the brains of normal bugs go where Jeremy's brain went when he flipped out.

If that annoying fly Eugene could invent a piece of pie capable of creating superpowers, the world's smartest roach could surely create a chemical compound, a microwave signal, or something that would reproduce the Jeremy effect, until every bug in school became a bad bug.

Cornelius's spine tingled with evil excitement. Why stop at Brown Barge? Every bug in Stinkopolis would be susceptible, every bug in the world! Billions and billions and billions of bugs!

If Super Fly hadn't stopped him, Crazy Cockroach's video-game mind-control plan would've worked. But since most adults don't play video games, his victory would've been limited.

The roach's 9,000-times-enhanced brain danced an evil mental jig. Once discovered, the Jeremy Effect would allow the super villain to achieve ultimate victory: Control over every bug on Earth!

6

Vicious Bugs

Meanwhile, on the good side of the diaper, Eugene and Fred discussed Jeremy's  outburst over a game of *Sewer Invaders*. The heroes' hangout didn't have a Ping-Pong table or mini fridge, kind of a sore point.

Fred caught an alligator in an electronic loop. "Do you think something like that could happen to us?"

Eugene kept his eyes on the screen. He didn't like to think about Fred's recent defection. Had his friend gone all . . . Jeremy? Changing his name to Furious Flea, doing all kinds of evil stuff with that Fiona. And hanging out with Cornelius and the Dungs!

Fred waited for an answer. "Well?"

Eugene blustered. "Nah. You heard Jeremy's rant. We don't have any bullies troubling us, nothing wrong with our siblings."

Fred agreed. "Elle's great. And everything's okay with the Flea family these days."

"We're getting enough sleep, doing well in school, eating right, exercising, and not overworking," Eugene added. "So nah, I don't think we'll be flipping out like Jeremy . . ." His voice trailed off as the game became more exciting. "Unless we let these alligators take over the sewers!"

By the next morning the super friends had put the strange incident out of their minds. Eugene and Fred expected a normal day at Brown Barge Elementary School.

But they hadn't even made it halfway down the hall when Ted Tarantula and Sid Spider suddenly pounced on the super buddies! Even with 9,000-times-enhanced strength, Super Fly and Fantastic Flea felt the barrage of blows delivered by sixteen furious feet.

Eugene shouted, "Hey, Ted! Stop that!"

Fred cried, "Sid! What're you doing?"

Eugene looked in Ted's eyes. They were wild with anger!

Sid snapped his jaws right near Fred's face. The super flea jumped out of the bully's grasp. Without his superpowers, the attack would've been disastrous!

Fred exclaimed, "Sid, that was vicious!"

Ted and Sid weren't the nicest spiders at Brown Barge. In fact, they were always kind of nasty. But this savage attack took their nasty to a whole new level.

Instead of backing off, the two crazed spiders grabbed Fred and Eugene and stuffed them upside down in trash cans. Both struggled not to expose their superpowers.

 Eugene rocked his can over so he could crawl out. His eyeglasses sat crookedly on his face. His antennae were dented.

Lucy Kaboosie cried, "Ted! That was so mean!"

Fred's back legs kicked helplessly. Lucy and Elle gently lowered his trash can to the floor. Fred backed out and brushed himself off.

Eugene straightened his glasses and stretched the dents out of his antennae. "That was weird!"

Fred looked thoughtful. "As weird as Jeremy's outburst yesterday."

Elle asked, "Coincidence?"

Eugene shook his head. "I don't think so. But that's about all I know." Eugene cleaned his eyeglasses. "Let's keep our eyes open and see what we can find out."

Elle nodded. "All facets."

Fred pointed down the hall. Sid and Ted had turned over every trash can, spilling garbage all over the halls.

 When the janitor told them to pick up the trash, Sid grabbed his broom and hit him over the head.

That's when everyone started calling the vicious spider Sid Vicious. Ted didn't earn a new nickname, unless you count, "Oh no! It's Ted!"

Eugene and Fred resolved to stick together and keep a careful watch on Elle.

"We can't reveal our superpowers!" Eugene whispered urgently.

Fred and Elle agreed. Maintaining a secret identity was vital to all superheroes. Without it, their nearest and dearest would become targets. Bad guys seek revenge!

Elle saw an orange spot on Eugene's shirt. She licked her feeler and rubbed at it, the way Mom did when she saw a stain but wasn't near a sink.

Eugene sighed. Then he looked puzzled. "I didn't have orange juice this morning. When did that stain appear?"

Elle rubbed her feeler on the stain, and then she licked it again. She tilted her head. "That's not orange juice."

Fred pointed to his shirt. "There's a spot—no, two—on mine."

Eugene smiled. "Don't wash your shirt. We'll test it in my lab after school."

Super Fly was right to suspect the orange drops had something to do with Ted and Sid turning vicious. Crazy Cockroach had concocted the orange potion and given it to the nasty spiders just before their hallway rampage.

Ted and Sid didn't question the juice boxes. Cornelius was always giving things away, like video games. Oh yeah, those were part of a mind-control scheme. But juice boxes...

Okay, the boys weren't the brightest spiders in their mothers' egg sacks. They were thirsty. The juice tasted great. And the next thing they knew, they were running wild!

The cockroach's formula made brain cells fire at an overwhelming rate, like when Jeremy popped his top.

Cornelius quietly experimented with several schoolmates, like Harrison Hornet, Nate Gnat, and Larry Leech. The juice seemed to darken

their already somewhat nasty natures. But it didn't have as dramatic an effect as it'd had on Ted Tarantula and Sid Spider.

Cornelius wondered why his freak-out formula worked so fast and furious on the arachnids. Maybe their eight-legged metabolism processed it faster? The brilliant roach would have to test further.

He soon discovered that the Jeremy Juice worked quickly on dung beetles too. Before the first bell, Doo and Dee destroyed an entire bathroom.

By lunchtime, Cornelius concluded that the badder the bug, the quicker the potion worked.

So far he'd succeeded in turning somewhat nasty or *Hyde*-like bugs into real scary **HYDES**.

To turn a good bug, or *Jekyll*, into a Hyde would require a stronger formula. He could do that. It was times like these that Cornelius really loved being 9,000 times smarter than just about every bug on the planet.

7

Bugs Gone Wild

Before you could say, "Sure, I'd like a juice box," half the bugs at Brown Barge Elementary School were running wild in the streets!

Super Fly's test on the orange spots had proved only two things: the compound tasted sweet, and it came clean with ordinary detergent. There simply wasn't enough present for even the smartest fly to determine the mixture's effects or ingredients.

Eugene sighed. "Someday Super Fly will have a better lab."

Fred looked around his friend's room, which was crammed with equipment. "Meanwhile?"

Eugene shrugged. "Let's see if we can get a bigger sample and try to keep some order on the streets."

That task quickly proved to be quite a challenge, even for Super Fly, Fantastic Flea, and Fly Girl. Everywhere they turned, bugs their age were going crazy, destroying public property, causing danger to themselves and others.

Elle stared at the mayhem in disbelief. "Doesn't anyone have homework?"

Fred shook his head. "No video games to play? No hobbies? I love jigsaw puzzles. Don't you?"

Elle smiled. "They are relaxing. And

when you finally put in the last few pieces..."

Eugene floated past them on the tall shoulders of the bugsketball team. "Less talk and more heroing, please!"

Soon, despite the best efforts of the three superheroes, the entire dump was devastated by crazed elementary school students.

Eventually the exhausted heroes retired to the good side of the diaper. While patching their wounds, they pondered.

Fly Girl arranged the pieces of the puzzle. "Okay, let's assume Crazy Cockroach created the orange juice concoction causing this outbreak of mad mischief. Why? How? And what can we do about it?"

The only bug that knew the answer was on the other side of the diaper. Cornelius's lab had even more equipment than Eugene's. And, of course, a Ping-Pong table and mini fridge right next door, so the villain could relax and enjoy refreshing snacks while on break. (Not that Super Fly was jealous, much.)

Anyway, Cornelius was feeling awfully smug. His bad-bug formula was making bugs go bad big-time!

For whatever reason, the Jeremy Juice had its strongest effect on the arachnids. Ted Tarantula and Sid Vicious Spider had each started his own gang. Big Butch Recluse and Wanda Black Widow also gathered gangs of tough bugs wanting to make trouble.

Soon sticky webs decked the halls of Brown Barge Elementary like ghostly holiday decorations. Of course the purpose of the webs was to hold small bugs captive!

Meanwhile, Cornelius kept tweaking his sinister solution. He wanted it to work with the same potency on other insects as it did on the spiders.

First Cornelius tested a new formula on his fellow roaches. After several adjustments, he finally turned up the bully odometer on Big Paulie Palmetto Bug. Then the tree roaches, water bugs, and flying cockroaches all fell to his plans.

Soon, almost every bug in school showed signs of the Jeremy Jitters. Screams echoed through the chaotic halls. The once-peaceful elementary school seemed like a prison in full riot.

Before he could be stopped, Timmy Termite ate half of Mrs. Tiger Moth's desk. Marco Moth chomped through every coat hanging in the teachers' lounge. And even though everyone knew glowing on school grounds was illegal, Frank Firefly lit himself up like a Christmas tree.

Nate Gnat led a swarm through the cafeteria, causing paper napkins to fly in the air like confetti. Andy Ant and Adam Aphid

teamed up to steal all the sugar packets, while Larry Leech and his friends sucked up all the ketchup.

Harrison Hornet and Killer Bee demanded tribute from all the smaller bugs and soon sat on a pile of plundered desserts.

All their lives these bugs had tended to

be more naughty than nice. Everyone told them to "be good." Now, under the influence of the Jeremy Juice, these nasty bugs' predispositions came out, and they let their bad blossom and bloom.

They weren't just bad, they were bad, BAD, *BAD*! And it felt strangely good, at least at that moment. Of course, they were too busy having fun to reflect on one basic truth: evil always loses—especially when good stands up to it.

At the moment, good was overwhelmed and Principal Mantis was frantic. He had lost control of his school. "What's going on? When did Brown Barge turn into a charter school for vandalism?" Normally the fierce-looking mantid could quiet any hall or classroom simply by striding into view on his long, powerful legs. Even the most hardened bullies had been known to crack under his mysterious stare.

But now he found himself holding books over his head as he dashed from his office to the cafeteria. It was like running through a war  zone. The middle-aged mantis worried that he was losing his toughness.

Poor Mrs. Mosca didn't know whether to call the police or hop in her car and never come back. She loved this school and all its students of every species, but she loved her family more. And she was only three years away from a cozy retirement and pension plan.

The principal kept hoping things would improve, that the students would get over this wildness like getting rid of a parasite. Mr. Mantis didn't want to call for help. He didn't want Brown Barge to gain the reputation of a troubled school. It could affect his school budget. On the other forelimb, things seemed to be getting even worse!

The clever cockroach quickly figured out how to adjust the juice to affect even the most docile bugs, like ants and bees. Not many social insects attended Brown Barge. Most went to private military or honey-making schools.

Thanks to Crazy Cockroach's insanity-inducing juice, St. Apocrita's Military Academy attacked Honeycomb Tech in a full-scale war! Their teachers were helpless to stop them.

"This will go on your permanent record!" exclaimed a frantic professor of Pollen Studies.

"Who cares?" buzzed a brilliant bee who was once on the fast track for a Hivey League college.

The streets of Stinkopolis swarmed with angry ants: fire ants, army ants, and other species—all mad with rage. These were not brave soldiers defending their queen and nests. They were *Ants Gone Wild*!

Cornelius cackled with evil delight. Watching the hordes of furious ants gave him the idea he needed. At last Crazy Cockroach knew how to defeat Super Fly and Fantastic Flea!

When they heard him cackle, Cornelius's henchbugs wondered, "What is it? What's so funny?"

Crazy Cockroach pointed to the ants and said, "There's the answer."

Dee whined, "What's the question?"

Doo asked, "There's a question?"

Cornelius put a star next to the top entry on his Top Secret To-Do List: *Find smarter henchbugs*. Then he explained, "We're going to build an army of bad bugs. A huge army, an army that will so outnumber those flies and their flea friend that they won't stand a chance!"

8

Hoops Lets Loose!

The next day, Eugene saw Hoops at the edge of a crowd of bugs accepting free juice boxes from Cornelius. The evil roach gave away the juice every day, and Brown Barge's students flocked to the boxes like moths to a flame. Actually, Cornelius also had matches to attract the moths. And of course Marco Moth was first in line, seeing as he's a moth and all.

Eugene didn't want to risk Hoops's wrath, but he felt

compelled to warn the new student about the juice. He nervously approached the scary hornet as she pushed her way to the front of the line.

"Um, you may want to stay away from Cornelius," Eugene whispered. "He's a bad bug, and that juice . . ."

Hoops pushed aside a small mosquito to grab a box from Cornelius. She drank the contents in one gulp. Then she smirked and said, "Good, bad, it's all  relative. Cornelius doesn't seem so bad to me. And maybe I like bad."

Eugene stammered, "Um, just a friendly warning, since you're new to Stinkopolis."

Hoops grabbed a second juice box right out of a little ladybug's hands. "Maybe you shouldn't try so hard to be your brother's keeper."

Eugene felt confused. He didn't even have a brother. But she probably meant that he shouldn't even try to be nice.

Elle tilted her head thoughtfully and then whispered, "I know Hoops seems mean, but I kind of like her."

Perhaps Elle sensed something about Hoops. She wasn't exactly evil. Hoops liked being cruel and violent, like an evil bug. But she really enjoyed putting down bad bugs, proving she was stronger than the bullies. Sometimes Hoops dreamed of becoming a cop, or a superhero like Fly Girl—only with cooler shoes.

Sadly, Hoops didn't stay likeable for long. After only a few days of drinking the Jeremy Juice boxes, the hornet became incredibly violent. She walked down the hall punching every bug within reach right in the face!

Thanks to their super speed, Eugene,

Fred, and Elle managed to avoid her ferocious fists. But Adam Aphid wasn't so lucky.

"Shee punnnched mee in da nose," Adam wailed in a nasal whine.

Eugene hesitated. As a hero, he felt obliged to defend all weaker bugs from that kind of violence. But he also had to protect his secret identity—and his nose!

That afternoon, on the good side of the diaper, Eugene and Fred discussed the Hoops question. Eugene began, "We can't let her go on beating up everyone in her path."

Fred agreed. But even with 9,000 times the strength of an ordinary flea, Fred felt reluctant to take on the hostile hornet. "I guess we could say something to her."

Recalling their conversation at the juice box line, Eugene felt skeptical. "We might have to do something more than talk."

"I wouldn't want to hurt her," Fred replied.

Eugene looked thoughtful. "I'm sure we can find a way to restrain her that wouldn't do any damage."

Fred nodded. "This could be a chance to test that power net you've been working on."

Eugene brightened. "You're right! I'll pack the prototype in my backpack tonight."

9

The Happy Hornet

The next day, Eugene didn't get to test his Nonviolent Power Net Restraining Device (patent pending). Hoops wasn't absent from school. She was . . . **NICE**!

Eugene, Fred, and Elle noticed the change immediately. Instead of punching every bug she passed in the hall, Hoops smiled. And it wasn't a snide smile or an evil smirk. This was a sunny, happy smile.

When Hoops smiled at

him, Eugene automatically smiled back. Then he wondered, what's going on?

Fred and Elle stared in disbelief. What was Hoops up to? Could this unexpected niceness have something to do with the Jeremy Juice—or was it just an unrelated change?

So far, Eugene's research on the Jeremy Juice had been unsuccessful. The trace amounts of juice left in each box didn't add up to enough of a sample for thorough testing. And Cornelius was very careful to make sure that Eugene, Fred, and Elle were *not* given boxes.

The bugs that drank the juice liked it so much they weren't inclined to share. And if they drank enough of it, they became so mean they wouldn't share anything ever.

Eugene looked down the hall at all the formerly nice bugs beating up one another, tearing up homework, throwing books, and otherwise acting out. Hoops glided past them all, smiling like she'd just won the Miss Bugaverse contest.

Eugene felt the first tingle of a very intriguing theory. He whispered to Elle and Fred, "Let's have a secret meeting after school."

It wasn't really necessary to be so formal. The three superheroes usually hung out after school anyway. And since they were the only ones attending the meeting, it would be secret to everyone else. But Eugene enjoyed calling secret meetings almost as much as Fred and Elle enjoyed attending them. It sort of comes with the superhero territory.

Of course first they had the daunting task of surviving another day at Brown Barge. Thanks to the devastating effects of the Jeremy Juice, everywhere they turned the heroes saw chaos!

Despite their dazzling reflexes, it was a long, painful day. Fred was so busy defending himself against Sid Vicious that he didn't see a rampaging wasp until it was too late to avoid his sting.

A moody grasshopper knocked down Elle, and while she was on her back, a bunch of beetles spun her around until she got horribly dizzy.

A pack of mites surrounded Eugene. He tried so hard not to hurt any of the tiny bugs, he tripped over his own feet and fell flat on his face.

Meanwhile, all around them battles raged. Hornets fought bees. Wasps battled yellow jackets. Spiders attacked roaches. And bedbugs fought one another fiercely while still wearing their pajamas.

On the playground, "General" Cornelius C. Roach commanded organized lines of fighting bugs. Platoons and battalions all followed his every command.

Eugene shook his head. "This isn't good."

Fred agreed. "Tell me about it."

Elle echoed, "Cornelius with an evil bug army—that's scary!"

In the interests of intelligence gathering, the three heroes listened to the general's speech to his troops. It made no sense!

Elle rubbed her forehead in distress. She said, "He's completely . . ."

"Crazy? As in Crazy Cockroach?" Eugene finished his sister's thought.

Then they noticed the villain's henchbugs. Doo and Dee were actually wearing helmets and uniforms!

Fred sighed. "Oh, brother! Look out for Captains Dee and Doo."

Eugene recognized the insignia. "No, they're colonels."

Elle declared, "They're numbskulls, and no amount of brass buttons, stripes, or salutes will ever change that."

Her brother and his friend chuckled. But the truth was that all three felt extremely worried.

As soon as their secret meeting was called to order, Eugene expressed his theory. "Maybe the reason Hoops turned nice after being so mean was because she was so mean to start with that a high dosage of the juice actually backfired."

Fred followed his friend's thought. "Hoops could only get *X* amount meaner before **BOOM**! she went back to nice."

Elle's skepticism gave way to interest. "You're saying that the juice had a reverse effect on Hoops because she's already mean? That's crazy! But so is Crazy Cockroach, so maybe . . . it's at least worth considering."

Eugene turned up the flame on his Bunsen burner. "And worth using as a basis for devising an anti-Jeremy potion."

Tattletales

Developing the cure for Crazy Cockroach's evil juice boxes could take some time—even for Super Fly, Fly Girl, and Fantastic Flea. So the three desperate heroes made a tough decision.

Eugene sighed. "There are just too many bugs to go against."

Elle agreed. "An entire evil army!"

Fred also thought the odds seemed grim. "Maybe we need help."

Elle nodded. "No one likes a tattletale,

but there are times when you just have to tell."

They started with Mrs. Flystein.

Eugene began, "Mom, there's something weird going on."

Elle continued, "Brown Barge has become a breeding ground for evil invaders!"

"The students have been brainwashed by juice boxes full of a diabolical potion created by Crazy Cockroach!" Eugene added.

Mrs. Flystein sighed. "I don't mind you playing pretend games after your homework's done, but I'm busy! Honestly, you make me want to cut off the cable TV."

Eugene felt horrified! Every now and then his parents threatened to save money on entertainment, but . . .

Elle wailed, "No! Please!" She loved her cartoons, especially those on Tick at Nite.

Mom shrugged. "Well, that's enough nonsense for now."

During supper, the young Flysteins tried again. Maybe Dad would be receptive and see the danger.

Instead, their father insisted that all the bad behavior at school could be explained by "prepubescent hormones. Lots of larvae  and nymphs act wild under the influence of the strong chemicals in their changing bodies."

Before Dad could launch into another version of "the talk," Eugene grumbled, "Never mind." Then he whispered to Elle, "Maybe Mrs. Tiger Moth or Principal Praying Mantis will listen to us."

Elle agreed.

So the next morning, the heroic siblings and their trusty friend Fred rushed off the bus. They dodged a gauntlet of bad bugs and finally reached Mrs. Tiger Moth's classroom.

The three tried to sound as reasonable as possible. Fred began, "Mrs. Tiger Moth, I'm sure you've noticed something strange is happening at Brown Barge."

Elle continued, "Some bugs are naughty, but this is ridiculous!"

Eugene concluded, "We believe many students have been brainwashed by Crazy Cockroach!"

Mrs. Tiger Moth said, "Principal Praying Mantis is, of course, aware of the . . . situation. Unfortunately, he's taking a wait-and-see attitude. And there's nothing I can do."

So the three heroes hurried to the principal's office. His response matched those of Mr. and Mrs. Flystein. He declared Eugene's theory "nonsense," and he blamed the wild behavior on puberty.

Worse than that, Principal Praying Mantis said he didn't appreciate Eugene, Fred, and Elle "telling tales."

Elle fumed. "We're not tattletales!"

The principal was quick to appease her. "Of course not. You're just telling on your classmates out of concern for the school. But I think our administration can handle any situation that arises."

Eugene shook his head. The halls had turned into a war zone, but obviously Principal Mantis preferred pretending that everything was fine. It was probably easier than facing his fears. Unable to control the chaos, he hid safely inside his shell, behind his closed office door.

The three heroes couldn't help feeling disappointed.

Eugene sighed. "That was useless."

Fred looked at his watch. "Worse than useless."

Elle sighed.

As the three heroes hurried to their classes, they passed Hoops Hornet. "Good morning!" she exclaimed with a sunny smile.

Hoops saw her reflection in the windowed top of a classroom door. She barely recognized herself.

Principal Mantis might be in denial. But Hoops knew that something strange was definitely going on at Brown Barge.

Hoops tried to adjust her face to its normal scary scowl. But in seconds that sunny smile returned.

Hoops couldn't understand it! She'd never felt so nice before. Usually she reveled in seeing bugs get hurt. She liked crushing bully bugs just to prove how much meaner she was. She lived to bully the bullies. But now all she wanted to do was be sweet.

Cornelius C. Roach watched the effects of his potion with great pleasure. Perhaps eventually Super Fly, Fantastic Flea, and Fly Girl would figure out a way to counter the Jeremy Juice. But with any luck at all, that would only be after his evil armies had done their damage.

Cornelius smiled slyly to himself. Soon all the bugs at Brown Barge would be turned against Eugene, Fred, and Elle. Life at school got ugly—fast.

11

Doubt

After another exhausting day defending themselves from their crazed peers, Eugene, Fred, and Elle collapsed in the good side of the diaper. The boys were even too tired to play *Sewer Invaders*!

Fred sighed. "Ted Tarantula and Sid Vicious are bad enough. Let's face it; they were always kind of rotten. But when good bugs like Grace Grasshopper and Lucy Kaboosie are acting like killer bees . . ."

Elle shuddered. "Lucy stole my lunch

today! Then she didn't even eat it. She just stomped on it on the floor."

Eugene shook his head sadly. "I wonder if this is it. I mean, maybe this is Crazy Cockroach's first plan that will work." He took off his glasses to rub his eyes. "Maybe it's our turn to fail. Maybe we're on the verge of losing Stinkopolis and the world! Maybe for once evil will triumph over good."

Elle looked alarmed. "Don't even say that!"

Eugene shrugged. "I don't even want to think it. But we're up against an awful lot of bad bugs."

Fred said, "Doubt is a horrible thing. We can't let fear or despair make us weak."

Elle casually lifted the coffee table over her head. "We're not weak."

The boys laughed.

Then Eugene said, "Perhaps it would be best to handle things as Super Fly, Fantastic Flea, and Fly Girl from here on out."

Fred and Elle agreed. Then while Eugene worked in his lab to find a counter-potion, Fly Girl and Fantastic Flea went cockroach hunting. Crazy Cockroach, that is.

After a quick check of the evil side of the diaper, the two heroes used their super speed to survey the entire area. They quickly found the vile villain at the highest point in the dump.

Fantastic Flea whispered, "What's he doing?"

Fly Girl shrugged. At that moment, Crazy Cockroach seemed to be doing nothing, just looking down on Stinkopolis. "Let's ask."

Cornelius saw no point in deceiving them. They would find out eventually anyway. So he told the truth. "I'm surveying my kingdom."

When the heroes looked blank, the roach added, "Surely you've heard the expression 'ruler of all he surveys.' Well, I'm surveying."

Fly Girl still felt confused. "Why? Why are you doing all this crazy stuff?" Of course, even as she asked, Elle realized "crazy stuff" was what Crazy Cockroach did!

Cornelius blithely explained, "I do this 'crazy stuff' because I can! Besides, it's the dream of every cockroach to rule the world. But I, I alone, have the means to achieve that goal!"

Then he laughed his horrible, cackling, crazy laugh before going on. "At dawn I will lead my army of bad bugs against the world. Soon everyone will see that my evil army is unstoppable!"

Suddenly the egotistical villain noticed Eugene's absence. "Where's the third loser in your tepid trio?"

Before Fantastic Flea could stop her, Fly Girl blurted the answer. "My genius brother is inventing an antidote to your evil potion."

The hills of trash and recyclables echoed with Crazy Cockroach's obnoxious laugh. The villain laughed loud and long.

"What's so funny?" Fantastic Flea finally demanded.

Cornelius shook his head. The

9,000-times-enhanced cockroach was too smart to reveal his formula's secret ingredient. Instead, he basked in the knowledge that, "Super Fly will never discover the secret of my formula. **NEVER**!"

Fly Girl shuddered. Could Crazy Cockroach be right?

The evil roach ranted on, "My plan will work. We stand on the brink of world domination!"

"Who's 'we'?" Fantastic Flea asked.

Crazy Cockroach grinned his ugly grin. "I speak in the royal we, as future King of the World."

Fly Girl looked around. "Oh, I thought you meant you and your witless assistants."

At that moment, Number 1 and Number 2 were busy filling juice boxes. At least, that's what they'd been doing when Crazy Cockroach left them. Knowing how reliable his henchbugs were, the villain muttered, "Perhaps I should check on the Dungs."

Crazy Cockroach didn't want to leave anything to chance. In the morning, the entire world would belong to him!

12

All Is Lost

The two superheroes spent most of the night trying to restore order to a town driven mad by the mad villain's insidious potion. By the time Fly Girl and Fantastic Flea returned to the lab, they discovered Super Fly passed out on the floor.

Elle felt worried. "Eugene, are you all right?"

Her brother didn't even bother lifting his

head off the carpet. "Just . . . exhausted," he replied wearily. "I . . . tried everything, and I still didn't find the answer."

"What are we going to do now?" a worried Elle chimed.

"But I did find the cure for stuttering," Eugene said proudly. "Notice I don't stutter anymore."

"You never stuttered in the first place, knucklehead," said Elle.

"Oh, then never mind," replied the exhausted superhero. "I guess we should start panicking now then."

Fantastic Flea tried to buoy his friend. "You will find the solution. You always do."

But Super Fly didn't feel so sure. Had that roach finally outsmarted him? He whined, "It was my invention that made him 9,000 times smarter. Why can't I figure out what's in his formula?"

Fantastic Flea and Fly Girl didn't know.

But they did have some scary news to share.

Elle began, "Crazy Cockroach plans to begin his invasion at dawn."

Eugene sighed. Time was running out! "We must do something!"

So the three superheroes spent the next hour brainstorming ways to stop Crazy Cockroach's evil army.

Fantastic Flea muttered, "There must be some way to trip them up."

Eugene briefly brightened. "Trip them! We could dump tons of banana peels beneath the feet of the marching army."

Elle asked, "Where would we get all those peels?"

Eugene drooped. "I don't know. Monkeys?"

"What about a giant shoe?" said Fred. "Like how Cornelius is always tripping the smaller bugs in school."

"Same problem. Where do we get a giant shoe?" asked Elle.

Then Elle suggested, "Maybe we can whip up a hurricane to sweep the evil army off its feet."

Fred liked that idea. "We could tell all the good bugs to stay inside."

Eugene felt discouraged. "One problem: how do we whip up a hurricane?"

The superheroes considered flying in circles to stir up a funnel cloud, then dismissed it.

"We'll probably just get dizzy," Elle reasoned.

Eugene agreed. "I don't think we could create a cloud big enough to wipe out Crazy Cockroach's whole army."

After a few minutes of head scratching,

Fred announced, "I've got a really far-out idea: let's fake an alien landing!"

Elle understood. "That might scare the evil army into running away."

Eugene loved the idea of fake aliens. But he fretted, "What if they don't run away? What if they attack our fake aliens? Besides . . ."

Fred finished for him, "How can we fake an alien invasion before sunrise?"

Discouraged, the three friends soon changed out of their superhero costumes. Their spirits were mighty low.

Eugene blamed himself. "Fred and I were having so much fun being best buds again, we neglected our superhero duties. We should've prevented our fellow students from drinking the juice boxes in the first place—instead of counting on creating a cure for Cornelius's evil formula."

Elle argued, "It's not your fault. Crazy

Cockroach had Number 1 and Number 2 working overtime on supply. Before we recognized the danger, there were just too many bad bugs to stop."

Not knowing what else to do, the three friends went to the school bus stop as usual. They were the only bugs there.

Elle observed, "Something's very wrong."

The three heroes looked all around. The only thing out of the ordinary was the lack of other students. Where was everyone?

Then they felt a rhythmic movement

beneath their feet. The ground shook like a drum under a steady beat.

Their enhanced hearing soon recognized the sound of many boots pounding the pavement. Crazy Cockroach's army was on the move!

In their spiffy uniforms, Number 1 and Number 2 commanded their regiments like real officers. But, our heroes wondered, whom were they going to attack?

Elle suggested, "I guess we'd better change back into our superhero suits."

In seconds, thanks to their super speed, the three heroes were back in spandex and flying high above Stinkopolis. The view was

alarming: huge hordes of bugs marched in unison.

Even at a glance, Eugene realized this was way more than just the student body of Brown Barge. Thanks to their super hearing, the three heroes soon had an explanation.

Number 1 and Number 2 had given all the Jeremy-Juiced bugs extra juice boxes to give their parents. So by the time parents wondered why their children were acting so strange, the parents had drunk the Jeremy Juice too. So the army grew, gulp by gulp, until it was massive!

By the time they neared the edge of the dump, Crazy Cockroach's evil army included almost every bug in Stinkopolis. The good and the bad were now all bad. And they were all under Cornelius's command.

Just as the three heroes wondered what they could do against such a massive army, they heard a voice calling out from below.

"What're you doing?" Hoops Hornet asked.

Super Fly replied, "We're superheroes, and our mission is to stop the evil army."

The tough hornet laughed. "Good luck with that." Then she added, "I'm going to school so I can have perfect attendance. Also, I want to be able to say there was one day when I was the smartest bug in school." Then she laughed again. "Because I'll be the *only* bug in school!"

When Hoops turned around, she almost ran into the Flystein and Flea parents. Before Elle had time to finish asking, "What're Mom and Dad doing here?" the heroes watched in horror as their parents joined the evil bug army. Super Fly moaned, "Someone must've given them the juice!"

Fantastic Flea clenched his fists in frustration. "What's in that stuff?"

Super Fly sighed. "I wish I could find out. That's the only way to counter its effects. But I'm not sure—and it's *really* bugging me!"

13

The Mad Mob

Super Fly flew to the front of Crazy Cock-roach's marching horde. He exclaimed, "I cannot let you leave this dump. Please don't make me hurt you, but I will not let you attack the outside world."

Crazy Cockroach laughed and laughed.

Various bugs threw garbage at Super Fly and otherwise demonstrated that they weren't afraid of him at all!

Rotten tomatoes and even rocks rained down on the brave hero.

Some started chanting, "Flies are stupid! Throw rocks at them!"

The mob turned on Super Fly, who had once been their darling. Fly Girl hid her face from the awful spectacle. Tears blurred Fantastic Flea's vision. All three wondered, how had it come to this?

Super Fly, Fly Girl, and Fantastic Flea stood shoulder to shoulder before the legions of bad bugs. They tried to push back the mindless mob, but there were just too many of them.

Their lips and chins dripped with the evil orange juice. The army left a trail of empty boxes.

Elle knew that often the best way to defeat a gang is to attack its leader. So Fly Girl flew straight at Crazy Cockroach, pounding him with her 9,000-times-enhanced fists.

Fantastic Flea jumped up and down on the heads of the Dungs.

The evil army laughed.

Super Fly flew in super-fast circles, trying to create a hurricane to stop the evil army. But the juice-crazed bugs marched right into the winds!

Fly Girl dug a trench to keep the horde from advancing. But they simply kept marching.

Fantastic Flea started doing flea circus tricks to distract the massive army, yet they still marched on.

Everywhere Super Fly looked he saw more juice boxes. Despair and panic threatened to defeat him as much as the evil army.

Super Fly feared they were beaten, that the roach had won. As the army grew bigger and bigger, it seemed the world would fall. Crazy Cockroach would soon become the King of the World.

And that's when Super Fly had his craziest idea yet.

Maybe he didn't need to know what was in the juice to make a counter-potion. Maybe what was in it would work for him as well!

14

Bad Bug Juice

Super Fly told Fantastic Flea and Fly Girl, "Follow me!" Without questioning, they took off.

Number 1 and Number 2 watched the heroes fly away and then turned to Crazy Cockroach.

Their leader sneered. "They're

running away because they're defeated and scared. They know they can't defeat my army!"

With his 9,000-times-enhanced brain, Crazy Cockroach easily grasped the irony of the situation. No one else in the world knew the secret ingredient that had eluded Super Fly. How could anyone know it was roach *tears*?

Roaches don't cry! But after continually losing to Super Fly, Crazy Cockroach had been so depressed tears had poured out of his eyes. The crafty villain mixed those tears into his bug juice, and that strange, rare ingredient turned the bugs that drank it into his helpless slaves. This time Crazy Cockroach would not be denied!

Crazy Cockroach flew high above the brainwashed bugs and began a big speech about "world domination and the coming new age of the roach, the year of the roach, the century of the roach, the millennium of the roach, the eternity of the roach, the double eternity of the roach, and the . . ."

Just then, Super Fly found the object of his search. Fly Girl and Fantastic Flea didn't understand. Why did Super Fly want a big batch of the Jeremy Juice?

Fantastic Flea wondered, "It's just more of the roach's crazy cocktail that turns good bugs bad and bad bugs worse."

Super Fly smiled slyly. "But it turned the WORST bugs good. Don't you see? We couldn't figure out how to make the counter-potion, but we have the poison and we know one cure for it . . ."

". . . is even more of it!" Fly Girl exclaimed as she suddenly grasped her brother's logic.

Fantastic Flea quickly agreed. "That's brilliant!"

On the front lines, Crazy Cockroach droned on about how "roaches will have the age of the roach, the infinite millenniums of the roach, and the era of the roach and will never be defeated."

Meanwhile, Super Fly, Fantastic Flea, and Fly Girl piled up box upon box of Jeremy Juice. Soon the boxes were so high the heroes had to be acrobats to balance them, super strong to carry them, and magic to see around them. They were bringing a whole lot of juice!

15

D-Day!

Finally Crazy Cockroach finished his super-long speech. He mentioned how bugs outnumber humans one billion to one, and with a brilliant leader like himself the human world was for the taking. He didn't so much conclude as run out of breath.

He pointed to the outside human world beyond Stinkopolis and howled, "**CHARGE**!"

Luckily, the long-winded

roach talked so long that Super Fly, Fly Girl, and Fantastic Flea had been able to bring all the Jeremy Juice back to the assembled army. They immediately began passing it around.

The evil bugs chugged the sweet juice. Listening to Crazy Cockroach had made them thirsty. Besides, they were addicted to the evil beverage.

"I said **CHARGE**!" Crazy Cockroach yelled again.

Number 1 and Number 2 charged.

But everyone else was too busy drinking the roach's delicious concoction.

Ba-WOOF, WOOF, WOOF! A loud series of barks echoed from the edge of the dump. A fierce junkyard dog took off after the charging dung beetles!

Fly Girl thought, "I bet that dog's going

to eat the Dungs!" Then she realized, "They deserve it."

At first Crazy Cockroach seemed oblivious to the mass mutiny. The frustrated general kept yelling for his troops to charge.

Then, when he realized his thirsty army kept drinking instead of marching, Crazy Cockroach went wild!

He flew down, grabbed bugs, and chucked them toward the outer banks of the dump. He tossed Timmy Termite almost a hundred yards. He tossed Ted Tarantula. He threw Sid Vicious Spider like a baseball!

Meanwhile, Super Fly's plan started working. As the concentration of juice in their bodies reached a high enough level, most bad bugs went back to their true, nice nature.

And the bugs who'd started out a little bit bad went back to being that, instead of mega-bad. At least they weren't brain-washed into following Crazy Cockroach anymore.

Since someone had to stop the bully roach from tossing bugs, Super Fly torpedoed himself into the villain's gut! **ZOOM! POW! SPRING!** Fantastic Flea jumped up and kicked the roach in the butt.

With the precision of a brain surgeon,

Fly Girl ninja-kicked him right in his roach nuts. **CRACK!** Together they crushed Crazy Cockroach with the worst beating of his life!

16

Peace in the Middle East (Middle East Section of the Dump, Anyway)

The next day, everyone was back to normal. All the Jeremy Juice had been guzzled, so no one was going back on the sauce anytime soon.

The town would've hailed Super Fly, Fantastic Flea, and Fly Girl as heroes, if they could remember what had happened. Unfortunately, it seemed all of Stinkopolis was suffering from a huge sugar-high hangover.

That was cool with our modest heroes.

Eugene, Fred, and Elle were happy just to be back in school and doing the stuff young bugs should be doing.

As for Crazy Cockroach, he was at home in a full-body cast. Roaches don't break easily since they have a pretty strong exoskeleton. Still, he'd gotten his butt kicked good!

And just to add insult to injury, Super Fly, Fly Girl, and Fantastic Flea all signed Crazy Cockroach's cast. It's not like the roach could do anything about it; he couldn't move or even talk.

So everyone was good. Well, everyone except Hoops Hornet. She was bad. And that was good—or, at least, that was the way she liked it.

Maybe someday Hoops would find her proper place in the bugaverse. In an ideal world, there'd be no need for violence and cruelty. But this was Stinkopolis. Sometimes bad bugs went wild, and you couldn't reason with them because they were completely crazy.

And they had to be stopped. So that's when you need superheroes, or good-bad bugs like Hoops, to kick evil's butt.

A few weeks later, Cornelius finally felt well enough to go to school. During recess, he was playing on the playground all by himself when a dirt cloud landed at his feet.

Cornelius turned around, expecting to see Doo and Dee, who'd been home with bad cases of pinkeye. Instead, he was surprised to see Ted Tarantula, Willie Weevil, Wanda Walking Stick, Adam Aphid, Andy Ant, Harrison Hornet, Nate Gnat, Larry Leech, Frank Firefly, Timmy Termite, Marco Moth, and Killer Bee all standing behind him.

"What's the deal?" asked Cornelius.

"We want you to stop," said Ted Tarantula.

"Stop what?" Cornelius demanded.

"Tricking us, using mind control video games, giving us Jeremy Juice potions, all the tricks you use to make us do what you want," said Ted.

Cornelius pretended to actually consider their request. "Well, I would stop, but I want to take over the world and become the supreme roach ruler. So I could lie to you and tell you I'll stop, if that's what you want to hear. But I won't. I'll never stop until the world is mine!"

"You're not getting it," Willie Weevil said.

"We like being bad," added Wanda Black Widow.

"You don't have to trick us into being bad," Ted stated.

"We *like* being bad," Willie repeated.

"All you have to do is ask," Wanda explained.

Cornelius took a minute to consider what they were saying. Was it true or a trick? There was only one way to know for sure.

Taking Wanda's advice, he asked, "You **LIKE** being bad?"

"We **LOVE** being bad," replied all twelve of the bugs standing in front of him.

"All twelve of you will help me take over the world?" the roach asked.

"We'll all help you take over the world," the twelve bad bugs declared in unison.

Cornelius looked at all of them. Twelve helpers, twelve assistants, all less stupid than the Dungs. His eyes almost filled with tears. Instead, he concluded, "Then you will be my Dirty Dozen. You will all become villains and do villainous things for the sheer joy of being bad—and with the express aim of helping me take over the world. Deal?"

"Deal!" shouted all twelve of the nasty bugs.

"From now on your villain names will be . . . Terrible Tarantula, Evil Weevil, Wicked Walking Stick, Awful Aphid, Angry Ant, Horrible Hornet, Gnasty Gnat, Loathsome Leech, Ferocious Firefly, Treacherous Termite, Menacing Moth, and Killer Bee," Cornelius announced, adding, "Killer Bee, your name is staying the same because it already sounds sinister and scary."

Killer Bee nodded. "That's cool."

If you think it's strange to know a cockroach can cry, it's even stranger to think a cockroach can smile. But that's what Cornelius was doing. That big bully roach wore a huge smile on his hideous face as he exclaimed, "To the dirty diaper!"

Cornelius took out his journal and wrote

on his Top Secret To-Do List: *Find a bigger hideout.*

So the thirteen evil bugs went off to secretly plan how to defeat Super Fly and take over the world once and for all!

Todd H. Doodler is the author and illustrator of the Super Fly series, *Rawr!* and the Bear in Underwear series, as well as many other fun books for young readers. He is also the founder of David & Goliath, a humorous T-shirt company, and Tighty Whitey Toys, which makes plush animals in underwear. He, too, is a part-time superhero and lives in Los Angeles with his daughter, Elle, and their two labradoodles, Muppet and Pickleberry.